Mary Louise Loses Her Manners

by Diane Cuneo   illustrated by Jack E. Davis

A DOUBLEDAY BOOK FOR YOUNG READERS

"Pass the pancakes," said Mary Louise.

"What do you say?" said Mother.

And Mary Louise said, "Pass the pancakes, poop."

Well, this was a shock to everyone. Especially to Mary Louise.

Mother passed her the pancakes.

"What do you say?" said Mother.

"Spank you very much," said Mary Louise.

"Excuse me?" said Mother.

"Excuse me?" said Mary Louise.

"What was that?" said Mother.

"What was that?" said Mary Louise.

"Are you mocking your mother?" said Father.

"Are you mocking your mother?"
said Mary Louise.

"Say you're sorry!" hollered Father.

Mary Louise tried to say, "I'm sorry,"
but instead it came out as "Burrrp!"

"Wow!" said her brother.

"You often forget your manners,"
said Mother. "But now I'm afraid
you've lost them altogether."

"Leave the table," said Father.
"And don't come back until you find them."

Where are *those manners?* wondered Mary Louise. She turned her pockets inside out. She shook her hair. She looked up her nose. Between her toes. Inside her shoes.

But they weren't there.

Mary Louise looked everywhere.

Maybe Mother is right, thought Mary Louise. *I've paid no attention to my manners, and now they've run away.*

So she went out for a look, and she took her wagon just in case.

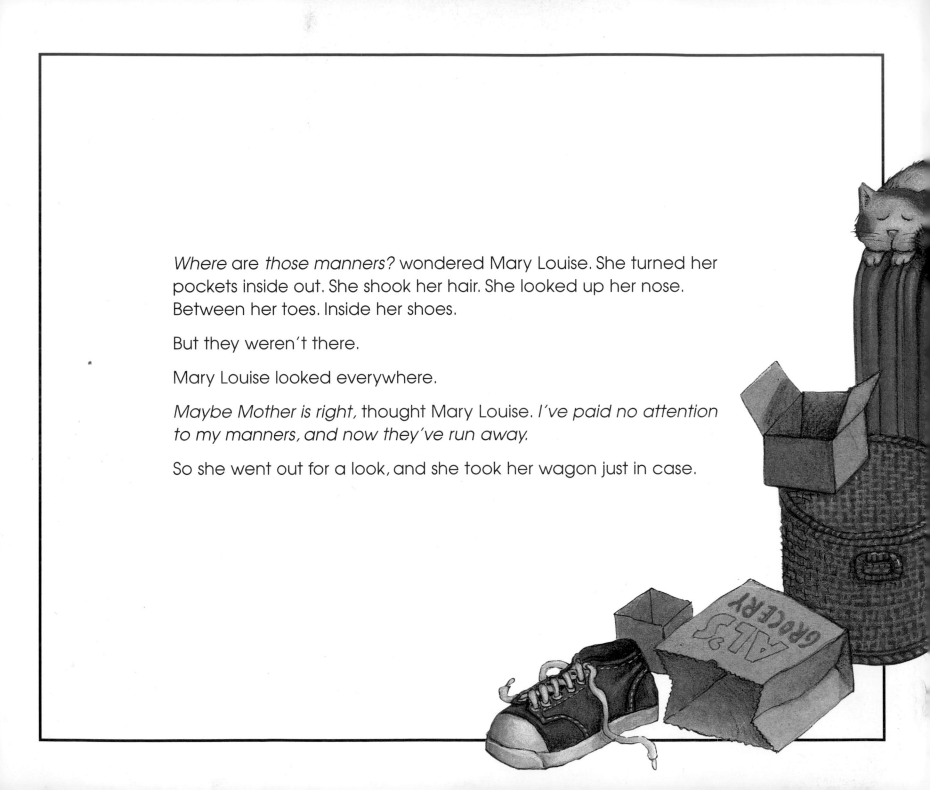

Outside, Mrs. Abby was at her easel, sketching and talking to Mr. Quicksberry.

"I've lost my manners," said Mary Louise, interrupting their conversation.

"Obviously," said Mr. Quicksberry.

"And I don't know how to find them," said Mary Louise.

"Can we help you?" asked Mrs. Abby.

"Yes," said Mary Louise.

"Yes, *please*," said Mr. Quicksberry.

"Yes, *fleas*," said Mary Louise.

"I see what you mean," said Mr. Quicksberry.

"What do your manners look like?" asked Mrs. Abby, flipping to a fresh sheet of paper.

"They have a big head for remembering all the rules there are about manners," said Mary Louise.

"And big ears for listening.

"And a little mouth to keep naughty words from slipping out.

"And no nose, for there's nothing polite about smelling and sniffing."

"And what about the eyes?" asked Mr. Quicksberry. "Are they always closed for going straight to sleep?"

"No," said Mary Louise. "They're stuck on long sticks for looking grown-ups in the eye when they're talking to you."

Mrs. Abby was drawing as fast as she could.

"They have very short arms," Mary Louise went on, "for not reaching across the table.

"And their hands have fingers as floppy as yarn for not pointing, since it's impolite to point.

"And they don't have feet, so there's no kicking or tracking in mud; but wheels instead, for when Father says to stop that lollygagging."

And after Mary Louise described the neat-and-fancy party dress her manners were most often seen in, Mrs. Abby proudly handed the finished drawing to Mary Louise. The portrait was perfect.

"Whack you," said Mary Louise.

"You're welcome," said Mrs. Abby.

And off Mary Louise went to find her manners.

At a nearby restaurant, the waitress recognized the manners in the picture. She said they had rolled in during the noon rush hour and helped put bibs on the babies and forks on the tables. The manners had said, "I hope you enjoy your meal."

"Would you like to help as well?" asked the waitress.

Mary Louise tried.

But instead of putting bibs on the babies, she put the bibs on the grown-ups—rather tightly.

And instead of placing the forks on the tables, she poked them into the babies, making the babies squawk.

"I hope you throw up your meal," she said sincerely.

The waitress sent her away. "If you hurry, you might catch up with your manners before someone loses her temper."

At the doctor's office, the nurse had seen Mary Louise's manners in the waiting room, handing out tissues and pills and saying, "Bless you," to everyone who sneezed.

"Would you like to help as well?" asked the nurse.

Mary Louise tried.

But instead of a tissue, she offered somebody a stinky sock. In place of pills, she handed out blue goo belly bombers. And instead of saying, "Bless you," she said, "Boogers."

The nurse sent her away. "If you hurry, you might catch up with your manners before someone calls the police!"

The hot-dog vendor had seen Mary Louise's manners toss a nickel into the street musician's case.

("That was *my* nickel!" said Mary Louise.)

The street musician had seen the manners turn the corner at Lackadilly and Vine with a little boy who needed help picking pansies.

The little boy with the pansies had said good-bye to Mary Louise's manners at the E Street bus stop.

And the bus driver said she had dropped off some very nice manners at the library.

Mary Louise wished she had exercised her manners more often. Maybe then they wouldn't have been running around town exercising themselves.

The library was very quiet.

"Hey! Who's in charge here?" yelled Mary Louise.

"Shhh!" said everybody.

"Come out, come out, wherever you are!"
Mary Louise hollered down the stacks.

"Shhh!" said everybody.

The librarian came up to Mary Louise. "You must be the girl who's lost her manners," she said.

"What's it to you?" said Mary Louise, as nicely as she could.

"Your manners are over there," the librarian said. "All tuckered out and sound asleep." She pointed at an odd-shaped heap covered with newspaper.

The heap heaved, very softly, in and out. "*Conk-cooooo! Conk-cooooo!*"

"I had to cover them," whispered the librarian, "because they snore."

Nobody's perfect, not even manners.

The librarian helped Mary Louise lift her manners into the wagon. Then, happy and humming to herself, Mary Louise headed back down the street. She promised herself that she would never give her manners a reason to run away again.

"Please," she said.

"Thank you," she said.

"Bless you," she said.

"Excuse me," she said.

"After you," she said.

"Lovely day," she said.

All the way home.

A Doubleday Book for Young Readers
Published by
Random House, Inc.
1540 Broadway
New York, New York 10036

Library of Congress Cataloging-in-Publication Data

Cuneo, Diane.
     Mary Louise loses her manners / Diane Cuneo ; illustrated
by Jack E. Davis.
          p.   cm.
     Summary: When Mary Louise starts saying things like "fleas"
and "spank you" instead of "please" and "thank you," she
realizes that she has lost her manners and goes in search of
them.
     ISBN 0-385-32538-X
     (1. Etiquette—Fiction.   2. Behavior—Fiction.)   I. Davis, Jack
E., ill.   II. Title.
PZ7.C91614Mar   1999
(E)—dc21   97-27875
                                                    CIP
                                                    AC

The text of this book is set in 12.75-point Avant Garde Book.
Book design by Trish P. Watts
Manufactured in the United States of America
September 1999
10 9 8 7 6 5 4 3   2 1
BVG

To my children,
Erik, Caley, and Rosalind,
and their friends
Chloe and Mimi Litman
— D.C.

For Annie and Alicia,
my well-mannered friends
— J.E.D.